TABLE OF CONTENTS

DEDICATION

This book is dedicated to the One I love, Whom I love because He first loved me and gave Himself for me— my precious Lord and Savior, Jesus Christ.

"O magnify the LORD with me,
and let us exalt His Name together."
Psalm 34:3

ACKNOWLEDGMENTS

Words could never express my heartfelt thanks and deepest appreciation to the following people:

Lenore Dickinson who "cared for my soul" and brought me to the cross of Jesus for cleansing from my sin by His precious blood.

Polly Newborg who has encouraged me to continue to "grow in grace and in the knowledge of my precious Lord and Savior."

Pam Creason—without whom this book would not have been possible. Our seventeen-year-friendship has been sweet. Her deep love for her Savior, her obvious God-given talent for writing, and her caring friend's heart have blessed my soul exceedingly.

Foreword

"I love them. I love the people."

I met Wilma Sullivan during the making of Catholicism: Crisis of Faith, a video documentary examining the teachings of the Roman Catholic Church. Before a camera in a peaceful rock grotto near Philadelphia, I asked Wilma about her years in the convent and how she had come to personal faith in Christ. My final question was: "Wilma, how do you feel about the Catholic people now?"

"I love them," Wilma answered without hesitation. "I love the people. But I'm sorry that the doctrines that they so cling to are not according to what God has said is necessary to get to heaven. My whole life has been given to help them to know the truth, the truth that can set them free."

I knew Wilma meant those words, that she really did love Catholics. The next day, however, I saw her love for them in action. We were scheduled to travel to New York City to conduct interviews outside Saint Patrick's Cathedral. Short of staff, I asked Wilma to join us.

9

The life of Christ shined through Wilma that next day. She greeted each person with a smile, caring for their needs as we conducted interviews on a busy Manhattan street corner. Wilma really did love these people. It was evident to us, and it was evident to the Catholics we met.

I thank God that now through A Sister of Mercy, others may come to know this remarkable woman and the work of God in her life. Here for the first time in print are the details of Wilma's call to service; her days in the convent, and how at last she came to experience God's mercy herself. May God use this book to His glory and through it lead others to salvation in the Savior.

James G. McCarthy
Director
Good News for Catholics

INTRODUCTION

During the time I was in the convent, I attended a retreat which included various instructional sessions led by nuns. In one of those sessions a nun led our small group in a discussion concerning Jesus' teaching in Matthew 9:13, "I will have mercy, and not sacrifice." She asked us, "What do you think it means?" The eight or ten of us in the group thought and thought, but none of us could come up with an answer. I believe I know the reason we were at a loss to comprehend the Scripture then. To us, sacrifice was the whole meaning of being a Sister of Mercy. We believed God wanted our sacrifice of service, our offerings of pity and compassion on people—and we couldn't comprehend mercy apart from those well-intended works.

Little did I know then that God was going to open up a whole new view of mercy in my life—God's mercy. Sure, having pity and compassion on other people is one form of mercy, but I learned that God's mercy is something far greater—totally undeserved, entirely sufficient, knowing no limits. God's infinite love reaches out in mercy to meet the needs of man in all his misery. "But God, Who is rich in mercy, for His great love wherewith He loved us," (Eph. 2:4) reached out and showed me that my sacrifice was not what He wanted; He wanted me to experience and enjoy His great mercy.

Serving God

Serving came naturally for me. I wanted to help everybody. As a child I cleaned around my house for my family on Saturday mornings, and then went to my neighbor's to ask them what I could do to clean their house. I was constantly looking for something that I could do for people. And from the time I attended parochial school, even in my early elementary years, my whole burning desire in life was to serve God.

Growing up as a Catholic girl in the 1950's, I thought that desire could lead to just one thing. The only way I knew how to serve God was to become a nun. Nuns were good; they were holy; they were mysterious; they were somehow closer to God. And since it was the only real way for a woman to serve in the Catholic Church at that time, becoming a nun resulted as the natural goal of my life.

The Sisters of Mercy taught me at St. Agnes Catholic School in my hometown, Towanda, Pennsylvania. I was on the convent steps early each morning to carry the teacher's book bag to the classroom. I cleaned the blackboards and did anything I could to make the nuns happy. Many people have childhood memories of their teachers, but nuns weren't just teachers. Back then they still wore the long, flowing habits with the coif and gamp. I watched in awe as they seemed to float along through the school halls. In childish wonder, I secretly wanted to lift their skirt hems to find out if they really had feet. I know other people who grew up around nuns sometimes remember unpleasant experiences, but these nuns emanated a positive aura in my early years.

Two of the nuns at St. Agnes had a special impact on my life. Sister Mary Ildephonse was my first grade teacher. Many children look up to their first teacher as a hero figure, and she certainly filled that role for me in her kind way. But an even greater influence was Sister Mary Josette, my teacher for most of my time at St. Agnes.

Sister Josette took a personal interest in her students, and that attention touched me. I loved sports, and she would get out and play baseball or catch with us in the school yard. She was more than just a classroom teacher, although she taught me all the basic school subjects. (I had a hard time with reading, but it wasn't her fault. I was too consumed with sports to want to read.) Her interest in me and in the sports I loved made me want to hang around her all the time. I stayed after school to clap the erasers, wash the blackboards, and do whatever I could to be around this person who was both warm and friendly and yet so mysterious at the same time. For several years Sister Josette not only kept me occupied and out of trouble, but also increased my desire to become a nun.

Though I left St. Agnes after six years, I did not leave the nuns' influence. My interests as a youngster included wanting to play various sports and wanting to become a cheerleader. Those goals put me in the public school, Towanda Valley Joint Jr./Sr. High School, for my 7th through 12th grade years. I graduated from there in 1962. Being in a public school, however, did not dampen my religious intentions. Catholic children like me, not attending parochial school, were required to attend Confraternity of Christian Doctrine classes (Catholic Sunday School) at St. Agnes with the nuns. On top of that, during Lent I went to Mass in the convent chapel every morning before school, and during the summers I attended some weekday Masses there. I often volunteered to help clean the chapel where the nuns worshipped. I swept the floor, dusted the pews, and cleaned an awful lot of candle wax off of things in the sacristy (the room where the priest changed into his vestments for the celebration of the Mass), but I counted it a privilege to serve in that way.

The nuns could be stern and strict, but I saw they cared and I wanted to be around them. They were good examples for me. I wanted to serve people and God like these ladies did, and so through those high school years my desire to become a nun grew.

At the end of my senior year in high school, just as my wish to enter the convent would have been ready to come true, I faced a personal tragedy that sidelined my plans. Right after Easter in 1962, my dad was diagnosed with cancer of the brain. Before he died he asked me, for personal family reasons, not to go into the convent right away, but rather to go to college. So I did go to Goldey Beacom College in Wilmington, Delaware, where I entered a two-year associates degree program. My second week in school there, my dad died. I idolized my dad, and his death was a devastating blow. But I carried out his wishes by staying at college and getting my degree in accounting and business administration.

There followed another detour on my road to the convent. After graduating, I went to work at the University of Virginia for two and a half years as a bookkeeper and secretary. There in Charlottesville from 1964-66 I reached out for spiritual guidance and for worldly pleasures at the same time. I went to Mass every day at the Neumann Center after work, but later I would go out to the disco club until midnight. Afterwards, I'd often go with a group to someone's apartment or house and party several more hours.

I moved to Philadelphia in 1966 to work as a secretary for the University of Pennsylvania, a move which ended up pointing my life back toward becoming a nun.

As I had in Charlottesville, I went to Mass every day at the Neumann Center. I met a nun there from the Immaculate Heart of Mary (I.H.M.) Order, Sister Evelyn Joseph. We talked after Mass often, and I told her about my lingering desire to become a nun. Because I had been trained in the Catholic school by the Religious Sisters of Mercy (R.S.M.), she counseled me to contact that Order. It was her friendship and help at that time that sent me back toward my life goal.

I did contact the Religious Sisters of Mercy, and it wasn't long before my desire was attainable. They had me come up to Dallas, Pennsylvania (near Scranton and Wilkes-Barre), where I went twice for meetings. Those meetings included interviews and psychological tests to make sure I was suited for convent life. The changes that were taking place in the Church and in the Order at that time prompted them to carefully examine applicants to make sure they were truly devoted to their calling, as well as mentally and emotionally qualified. I passed! And so on September 8, 1967, I entered the convent located on the campus of College Misericordia there at Dallas.

We had to take names as nuns, and I had been thinking that I would like to become Sister Vivian Aleen James, a combination of my mother's and father's names. Because of the changes of the Second Vatican Council of the Church (1962-65), however, the Order was asking us to take our baptismal name combined with a form of Mary. So instead I became Sister Wilma Marie, R.S.M. To be a Sister of Mercy seemed so appropriate. All I knew of mercy was the pity and compassion like that shown to me by the nuns in my childhood. I certainly wanted to show mercy by serving others, and now that was all wrapped up in my new name.

Because of my educational background, the Order began training me for administrative work in a hospital or school or for teaching business subjects. (The Sisters of Mercy were formed to be nurses, teachers, social workers, and administrators.) They had me go back to college my first (or postulant) year at College Misericordia to further my preparation. I took liberal arts courses that would supplement my business degree and worked part time in the registrar's office. Sister Mary Luke, my business teacher at the college, was an encouragement to me that year. She always had a listening ear when I needed to talk. Sister Mary Eloise, the registrar, was very demanding, but I worked hard for her in the office and we got along fine.

I found life as a postulant a time of adjusting, learning and serving. I was getting used to being in the Sisters of Mercy, going to school, and doing a lot of cleaning. The Order did consider that first year a time of adjustment to convent life, so they allowed a fair measure of contact with the outside world. My family could even visit me once a month. While there in the convent we learned lots of serving skills. One particular bit of instruction involved waiting on tables in the formal way required for a papal visit or a visit by a bishop, archbishop, or cardinal. Then there were the regular chores or "charges" that were assigned to us. We had to help the cook prepare meals in the kitchen, set tables, and serve meals to the other nuns. (I'll never forget a time when Sister Barbara, one of the other postulants, was serving a meal. She dropped an entire tray of dishes and food. The Directress of Postulants, Sister Aidan, made her clean up every bit, and she had to continue serving tables for a long, long time.)

We did lots of laundry and made a lot of beds. We worked in the large laundry room, learning how to operate the mangle, a big piece of equipment that pressed sheets. We learned to fold laundry items properly. We were assigned to take care of Sister Aidan's room. Sister Aiden was the Directress of Postulants; everything in the room had to be white-glove clean, and the sheets on her bed had to be turned down exactly right. If we fell short in any way, we had to keep that assignment for what seemed to be an eternity. (We may have been Sisters of Mercy, but we found little mercy in our Order if our serving skills did not meet rigid expectations.)

There were only four postulants in our "band" that year: Sister Virginia, Sister Barbara, Sister Victoria, and me. To make working in the convent a little more fun, we nicknamed some of the equipment we used. For example, "Sister Buffer Marie" was the big industrial buffing machine we used when we stripped and waxed floors. And "Sister Hobart" was the big dishwasher.

I may have entered a somewhat austere life as a Sister of Mercy, but I didn't have to give up my love for sports. I played tennis whenever I could there on the College Misericordia campus. I played in my habit with the old veil just a flying behind me. (Later, during my third year while I was teaching in Harrisburg, I joined a parish bowling league. One week I bowled the high game of 256. The Jewish man who owned the bowing alley refused to put my name as Sister Wilma Marie on the board across the lanes announcing the top male and female bowlers of the week. Instead I was chalked up as Wilma Sullivan.)

Though I certainly had some fun in the convent, a nun's life is supposed to be one of worship and piety. We had plenty of religious exercises to keep that focus clear. After daily Mass and breakfast, Sister Mary Aidan led us in morning devotions. We took different passages from Scripture, meditated on them and shared our thoughts with one another. I also had my private devotions and read the required prayers called the Office (which included Lauds in the morning, Vespers in the evening at the supper hour, and Compline at bedtime).

A peculiar part of convent life was the "night silences." From 9 o'clock at night until after breakfast in the morning, we were not allowed to talk at all, except in an absolute emergency. The nun assigned to knock on our doors to awaken us was exempted for that purpose, but otherwise we all kept silent. Of course the morning routine involved the Office and Mass before breakfast, and we could speak the required prayers in unison and participate in the Mass, but there was to be no talking in the halls or at breakfast whatsoever. The only times we were released from this silence during breakfast were on first class feast days. Those were Sundays and days of celebration like that of the Immaculate Conception of Mary on December 8 or other holy days of obligation.

There were lesser feast days. I had one of my own; it was May 7. I was baptized in the Catholic Church on May 7, and so, that was Sister Wilma Marie's feast day. If I had school classes that day, I had to attend, but I didn't have to do any charges. And, to help make the day special, the other nuns gave me a party. In essence, personal feast days replaced birthdays in the convent.

One incident sticks out as a memorable event in my first year at the convent, even if it seems a bit "unnunly." Sister Aidan was in charge of our postulant band, but when she wasn't there, as the oldest postulant at age twenty-three, I was the leader of our group.

One time when she went out of town for a conference, I decided to have Sister Victoria cut my hair (an act that required permission). She had been cutting hair for all of us that year. This time I decided to have her cut my hair short in a pixie style like I had worn before I entered the convent. When the canonical novices (second year nuns) saw me, they said, "Oh, are you in trouble! You are going to get killed by Sister Aidan!" The senior novices (third year nuns) joined in the warning. I soon started to get afraid, and the three other postulants and I tried to think of some way we could make my hair grow—fast. Of course it didn't, and Sister Aidan returned. She was absolutely furious, and following a big lecture, I was just as mad at her. We spent the next three days giving each other the silent treatment. Then she had me come into her office where we stared at each other for a while. After some more lecturing, she said, "You'd like to swear at me, wouldn't you?" (She knew I had a swearing problem before I entered the convent.) I looked at her a while and then replied in the affirmative. She said, "Well go ahead." So I did! We both laughed, and it was over.

Though I was far from being a perfect postulant, I was still intent on serving. Every Saturday night I would collect the shoes of the nuns who lived on my hallway. I lined them all up in the laundry room and polished until my fingernails were black. I loved helping others, and all those shiny shoes at Mass the next morning made me feel like I had served God in a unique way.

My second or canonical novice year was one of greater seclusion and spiritual training. Most of my time was spent at the convent in religious pursuits such as studying the life of Christ and the documents of the Second Vatican Council. And of course, I did a lot of cleaning—it helped me keep my mind off not having visitors as often that year.

The four of us from the postulant band continued on together as canonical novices, but we gained five more from other convents. Because of the smaller numbers of nuns entering religious vocations and the great expenses involved in operating convents, some were closing. Sisters Rita, Julie, and Stephanie transferred to us from Nebraska, and Sisters Cecilia and Madeline came from Mother Teresa's order in India.

I had an interesting experience at the convent one

afternoon that year. At the time it seemed insignificant and unmemorable. I was walking through the recreation room which contained the television. It was not supposed to be on during the day, but it was. No one was around. And speaking there on the screen was Billy Graham. He was concluding a message and giving an invitation. I stopped momentarily and listened. I remember thinking to myself as I heard him speak, "God, I want what he's talking about." I walked on out of the room and didn't think about that experience again until several years later.

My career as a nun took a sudden turn at the beginning of my senior novice (third) year. I was supposed to go back to school and finish my college education, but the Sisters of Mercy had an emergency that changed everything. A nun from Our Lady of the Blessed Sacrament School in Harrisburg, Pennsylvania, was killed in an automobile accident two weeks before school was to begin. Someone was needed to teach her second grade class, but the slate (the assignment sheet for all the nuns) had already been posted, leaving no teachers available. They asked me, since I was nearly finished with my education, if I would fill the position. I agreed and moved immediately to the convent in Harrisburg.

This new opportunity for service found me willing but not exactly prepared. I was suddenly teaching second graders in a self-contained classroom, but I had no elementary education training at all. I didn't know enough about phonics to teach the children on my own, so I got help. Another nun in the convent where I lived, who had taught my students the year before in first grade, taught me enough phonics each night to get me through the next day's lesson with the class. And there I was, one of worst readers in the world, teaching those kids reading. Somehow I survived, and I even agreed to teach again the next year—a year that was to be my last as a nun.

DISILLUSIONMENT

On June 19, 1970, during the summer between my two teaching years at Harrisburg, I took my first vows as a Sister of Mercy. I had returned to Dallas for the summer, and there I committed myself with these words: Lord, at Baptism you called me to be, only in terms of you. Today, as a Sister of Mercy of the Union, I desire to emphatically strengthen and actualize my consecration of Christian witness. I come before you, Lord, to lay down my life that, one with you and with your people, I may take it up again. In keeping with the Mercy commitment to the Church and to the world, and through fidelity to your will for the sake of the Kingdom, I, Sister Wilma Marie, promise to this congregation dedicated to Mary, to accept the responsibilities of a life of consecrated celibacy, poverty, obedience, and service to God's poor, sick, and uneducated. . . .

I took my vows very seriously, knowing the promise I was making before God. Yet even as I took them, a troubling issue was weighing heavily on my mind.

The 1960s had been a turbulent time for monastic orders because society was changing rapidly, and the Church was struggling to stay relevant and appealing to Catholic young people. No longer content with the strict religious life, many nuns were leaving the convents (and priests were leaving the priesthood). In recognition of the turmoil and the possibility of defection, the Order had me take my vows to the Sisters of Mercy and to God, of course, but not to the Church hierarchy (the Pope, a cardinal, or a bishop). And, as a further precaution, those first vows of mine were taken for a limited period of time, three years.

Actually, I was thrilled with the changes the Church was making in that era. Vatican II had changed the Mass to be spoken in English instead of just in Latin. The priest, who had always had his back to the people, now turned around to perform the Mass facing the people. The high church music could now be joined by more contemporary music. Even our required prayers (Lauds, Vespers, and Compline) were in English so that we could understand them. The updating made worship more interesting, and I loved it.

But along with those inspiring changes in the Church, I also saw changes that I questioned—changes in the lifestyle of the nuns. When I moved to Harrisburg in 1969 to teach, the convent there was an experimental house which allowed greater freedom to the nuns than they had experienced in the past. There was no mother superior over the house as there had been in the "old days." All six of us who lived there would sit down and decide together who was going to do what charges or chores.

Along with that organizational freedom, however, several of the nuns were taking additional liberties in more spiritual matters. One of the nuns didn't want to attend daily Mass, and no one made her go. Another didn't want to teach while wearing the new modified habit (the shorter dress with the shorter veil, which I thought was very comfortable and appropriate). I felt that if they were there to worship and serve God as nuns, they should be willing to go to daily Mass or to show that they were representing God and the Sisters of Mercy by wearing the habit. And there were several other things happening there that I saw as hypocritical to our calling as nuns as well as being in violation of our vows before God. Dealing with those situations so close around me disillusioned my lofty expectations for life as a nun.

When I took my vows that summer at Dallas, I shared my concerns with my superiors. They gave me the option of staying there and going back to college that next school year or returning to Harrisburg to teach second grade again. I knew that they really needed me to go back and teach, so I willingly agreed to serve again in that capacity. I was sure the problems could be worked out.

However, the problems were not worked out. That second year in Harrisburg my disillusionment grew as I faced additional troubling situations in the convent. In all sincerity, I wanted to serve God and be like those inspiring nuns I knew in my childhood. But the Harrisburg convent's loose organization allowed personality clashes and questionable situations to continue without resolution. I often found myself in arguments with the other nuns, and the tensions were straining my emotions. This just wasn't what I expected in a convent; it wasn't how Sisters of Mercy should be.

The emotional turmoil on one occasion brought me to the brink of suicide. After some heated words with another nun one afternoon, I left a note behind at the convent and went walking for several hours. (I changed into regular street clothing so I wouldn't be recognized.) I didn't want to talk with any of the priests at the church, so I went to a nearby hospital, hoping to find a chaplain or someone there to talk with. By then it was evening, and they all had left work for the day. I then walked over to the Susquehanna River, two blocks away from the convent. I stood there looking into the river and contemplating taking my own life. I stood there for a long time, but I couldn't do it. After a while I walked up the street a few blocks to a college building that was open. I found an empty classroom, sat down, and tried to pray to God. There seemed to be no answer to my confusion. Finally, about 9:00 p.m. I went back to the convent. The nun with whom I had quarreled had found my suicide note. On my return she started to pick a fight again. In my despair and irritation, I told her to "Get off my case!" I was really angry, and she realized it. She backed down and went to get me some supper, ending the incident but not my predicament.

Shortly after that traumatic experience, I contacted the Mother Provincial in Dallas and asked for a leave of absence from the Sisters of Mercy. She was very understanding, asking if I'd like to go somewhere and pray before I left. I said, "Yes! I don't really want to leave, but I just see too many things that are hypocritical." She took care of the details, finding a replacement for my teaching responsibilities and sending me to a convent in Johnstown, Pennsylvania, where I could pray and spend time alone sorting things out.

I stayed in Johnstown five weeks, but the time added to my frustrations rather than soothing them. While there, I got involved in the newly emerging Charismatic Movement of the Catholic Church. There were priests and other nuns as well as lay people attending lively meetings in a church basement in nearby Ebensburg. After singing a lot of "feel good" songs, they began speaking in tongues. I went and watched, but in my confused state, I found the emotionalism of the meetings terribly upsetting. I found no answers, only added turmoil—so much so that I called the Mother Provincial again and told her that I just had to leave.

There was no hassle, no condemnation, only compassion for me from my superiors in the Sisters of Mercy. The Mother Provincial assured me that there wouldn't be a lot of red tape involved in releasing me from the vows I had taken. She made sure I had a ride back to Dallas, and when I arrived there I met with her and some other members of the Provincial Council. In that meeting they were very kind and understanding. I signed the papers to be released, and they gave me a check for two hundred dollars and some things to help me get settled again on my own. They even let me use one of their cars so that I could go home to tell my mother what had happened.

I left the convent on March 27, 1971 with no anger at all toward the Sisters of Mercy. They had indeed been merciful to me, showing me real compassion in my time of deep despair. When I returned the car I had borrowed to drive home to talk with my mother, they insisted that I spend the night there with them in Dallas rather than get a motel room. They also gave me a going-away party and told me that if I ever wanted to come back, all I had to do was pick up the telephone and call them. The kindness of those ladies was overwhelming, but their help just wasn't enough to overcome the spiritual dilemma I met in Harrisburg and Johnstown. I couldn't stay in the convent with things as they were. I would have to turn back on my lifelong goal of being a nun.

TALKING TO GOD

The parents of a college friend of mine at Goldey Beacom, Mr. and Mrs. Nolan from Lansdale, Pennsylvania, picked me up from the convent and took me home with them for my start in life as an ex-nun. I stayed with them about three weeks while finding a job and an apartment. I was hired as an executive secretary for a computer company in Ft. Washington, and the apartment I rented was in nearby Hatfield, located about an hour north of Philadelphia. Early in 1972 I changed to another job as secretary in a large center-city Philadelphia law firm, commuting an hour each way by train. I may have left the convent and become a regular working girl again, but I hadn't left my desire to serve God behind. I still sought solace and avenues for service in the Church, while I searched futilely everywhere else for something to give my life meaning and fulfillment. When things got overwhelming, I found myself talking to God.

I desired to be active in the Catholic Church, not just attending weekend Masses, but also participating in every way I could. For about a year I taught music at the Saturday night and Sunday Masses at the Catholic Church in my Hatfield parish. I'd walk up and down the aisles, leading the music and helping people learn the new songs we were singing then. Later I started attending St. Stanislaus Catholic Church in Lansdale. I was dating a man named Steve, who attended Mass there and taught in their school. He and another friend of ours, Louise, and I enjoyed doing things together, including going to St. Stanislaus. I got so involved in that church that they would have considered me one of the lay leaders, even though I wasn't a member. I sang in the choir, helped the priest with projects, and assisted in other ways in the church.

I stayed busy with friends and activities, but I was falling into the clutches of destructive habits. For two summers I was part of a large theater group, building sets, singing, and acting in plays held at Gwynedd-Mercy, a Catholic college north of Philadelphia. After working on play scenery or costumes, we'd go out to eat—and drinking was always included. I had always said that I would never drink alone, but before long I was finding myself keeping alcohol in my apartment and drinking there by myself. Besides having the alcohol problem, I was smoking heavily, swearing handily, and I was just about ready to fall into deeper ruin, had it not been for God's great mercy.

In November 1972, while working at the law firm in Philadelphia, I took a vacation to the West Indies, a vacation with an unexpected outcome. Having "fun in the sun" in Montego Bay, Jamaica, I began to think that my life was going nowhere as a secretary in a stuffy old office. Why not try something different and exciting? Why not see the world? So after my return home, I contacted the travel agent who had booked my tour, and I got the names and addresses for a number of cruise lines. I wrote and sent resumes, and in January I headed to Miami to work for the M/V Freeport Cruise Line.

For three months I sailed on three-day cruises to Grand Bahama Island, Nassau, and back to Miami. I worked in the Purser's Office, the ship's administrative office. I dealt with the people at the main information desk, answering questions, selling tickets for night clubs and casinos, and helping the passengers in many other ways. I also handled passports for foreign passengers (those who weren't US residents). Foreigners had to travel under the ship's "umbrella" in the Bahamas, and so we took their passports when they boarded the ship. Then we worked with them and the immigration officials to get them back into the US at Miami on our return. Both on duty and off, there were plenty of temptations, and needless to say, the cruise ship atmosphere did nothing to improve my moral morass.

Twice a week, Wednesdays and Saturdays, we docked in Nassau, and I went to Mass at the mission church, always staying afterward to quietly think and pray. The priest noticed my regular attendance and one day struck up a conversation as I was leaving. I happened to mention that I was using this Saturday Mass as my "Sunday obligation." (Until 1965 all Catholics were required to attend Mass on Sunday. The Vatican II changes, however, allowed the Saturday night "vigil" to be substituted for the "Sunday obligation.") To my surprise, he said, "You can't do that!" That change was implemented in the United States, and he readily informed me that Nassau was not in the United States. It was in the Diocese of the Bahamas, and I couldn't do it there. I tried to explain that there was no Mass on-board ship on Sundays, and I was doing all I could do. To my exasperation, he declared that he would not allow me to go to communion, nor would he hear my confession from that point on.

I left the church in bitter frustration and began talking to God as I walked back to the ship in the harbor. "God! That's not fair! I've done all that I can do to get to Mass. My job on the ship makes it impossible to go to Sunday Mass. But that priest is telling me I'm in mortal sin for not going on Sunday. It's just not right!"

Talking to God was not something new for me. Even as a girl growing up in Pennsylvania, when I faced a problem and no one seemed to understand what I was going through, I would go to the church. I'd sit in a pew all by myself and just talk right out loud to God. One of those situations I remember in particular was when an important dream of mine was shattered. My sister Marilyn, who is two years older than I, had been a cheerleader, and I was determined to be one also. Well, I did get to be a junior varsity cheerleader, but when I tried out later for varsity, I didn't make the squad. I was crushed, and like most teenagers in a personal crisis, I felt that no one understood or cared. So I headed over to SS. Peter & Paul Roman Catholic Church there in Towanda and talked to God about the situation. Somehow I knew He understood.

That's what I found myself doing again there in the Bahamas: not "Hail Mary, full of grace" or "Our Father which art in Heaven" or any formal prayer, but simply pouring out my heart to God. I didn't know it then, but while I was feebly trying to reach out to God, He in His wonderful mercy was preparing to draw me to Himself.

FINDING MERCY

My adventure on the high seas turned out to be a disappointment. I tired of the same ports over and over again. I longed for the good old solid trees of Pennsylvania instead of wispy palms. I missed my family and friends. Before three months had passed, I gave the cruise line my two weeks' notice. But one day during those last weeks, while I was standing at my desk I experienced a tremendous pain in my abdomen. I doubled over in agony. The ship's doctor checked me out, but he couldn't do a detailed examination there on board. He thought I might have some tumors and advised me to see a surgeon when I returned to Pennsylvania. As it turned out, the Lord was going to use my medical need to lead me to the answer for my spiritual disillusionment and desire.

In April 1973 I headed back north to my old apartment in Hatfield (which I had sublet to some friends while I was gone), a new job at a Lansdale law firm, and my old lifestyle. But I had that new ailment. I went to see a surgeon, and he confirmed that I did have tumors, but he tried to see if medication (estrogen therapy) would control them or even take them away. By the end of October I was reacting to the medication, and he had to put me in the hospital for surgery.

While in the hospital I had a Catholic roommate who enjoyed listening to the stories I could tell. On the morning of my surgery I was relating tales of my convent days, my cruise days, and my disco days (my old dancing days back in the '60s while at the University of Virginia). I didn't realize that my colorful accounts could be heard all the way across the hall in another room, but someone else was listening in. (It has been said that I have a "mega-

phone mouth," and in that case it must have been true.)
A lady who had been confined to her bed got so involved
in my stories that she was laughing just as much as we
were in our room.

The lady across the hall was Lenore Dickinson, and
against doctor's orders, she got out bed and came over to
our doorway. When I saw her and she asked if I was
really an ex-nun, I was taken back a little because I didn't
have a clue as to where the woman had come from. She
apologized and explained that she could hear me from
her bed across the hall and that she was curious about
what I was saying. So I confirmed that I really was an ex-
nun, and with her propped in the doorway and I and my
roommate still in our beds, we went right on talking. And
as we conversed, the nurse was coming in and out of the
room getting me ready for surgery, but she was not pay-
ing any attention to who was standing there by the door.

Before they rolled me out for the operating room,
Lenore found an opportunity to ask me something.
"Would you mind if I asked you a personal question?"
Of course, I indicated that she could go ahead. "If you
would die in surgery today, do you know 100% for sure
that you're going to go to heaven, without any doubts at
all?" My thoughts in response were totally positive. I
was going to daily Mass; I was involved in my church; I
was doing the best I could. Besides, even if I wasn't perfect, I was always told by the nuns (especially since
Vatican II) that it took a bad person to go to hell and that
God is a God of love. So I offered the obvious response—
"Well, sure I do!" At that very point, the nurse in the
room finally noticed Lenore and ordered her back to bed.

After my surgery, Lenore and I had opportunity to
chat more. We were both practical jokers, and we combined wit to pull pranks on her gullible husband and some
of our other visitors. We enjoyed the laughs together,

and when I was discharged, we exchanged names, addresses, and phone numbers. For the next week we called back and forth to find out how each other was feeling. Then, she wrote me a letter to ask if I would come and talk with her about spiritual things. Now I knew that she was in the hospital before I got there, and she had to stay in longer after I left. And I knew that she knew that I was a former nun. I concluded that she must have cancer, and she needed someone to talk to. So I called her up, thinking I was going to be a "Sister of Mercy" who could go talk to her and try to encourage her. However, it wasn't any need of her's that she was concerned with; it was mine.

Lenore invited me over to her house one evening for a talk, but she was afraid to deal with me by herself, at least initially. So she arranged for two of her friends to show up fifteen minutes apart while I was there. If she didn't have an answer for me from the Bible, maybe Barbara would; and if Barbara didn't, surely Anita would. She knew this ex-nun needed the Lord, and she and her friends were willing to do whatever it took to share Him with me. It took listening to me talk for three hours! (My dad always said I was vaccinated with a "victrola needle," because I just go on and on and on!) I talked with those ladies about the goodness of God, the love of God, and the service of God. I talked about my experiences as a nun, a cruise ship worker, and a disco dancer.

Finally, Lenore said, "Wow! Would our pastor like to meet you! You've said so many interesting things, particularly about your days as a nun. He was raised by nuns in an orphanage, and he would just love to meet you!" I surprised all three of them when I replied that I'd be glad to meet him. (Prior to 1965 it was a mortal sin for a Catholic to visit a church of another denomination. But because of Vatican II and the ecumenical movement in the Catholic Church, we were now encouraged to pray with people from other denominations and even allowed to visit their churches.)

So, on the next Sunday morning, I went to Mass at St. Stanislaus first and then to the service at their church, Calvary Baptist in Lansdale. There were two things about that church that really impressed me. The first was that there were over fifteen hundred people there, smiling and singing from the bottom of their hearts and the top of their lungs. I know I thought, "What have they got that I haven't got?" because I wasn't used to people really singing out in church. Rather than the drudgery of worship routine, these people had joy in their voices and on their faces. The second was the preaching of the pastor, Dr. E. Robert Jordan. He never quoted a philosopher or theologian like I was used to in the homilies (the priest's short— ten to fifteen minute—sermons during the Mass). I think Pastor Jordan quoted the Bible from Genesis to Revelation and all the way back again that day. And even more amazing to me was the fact that when he quoted from Scripture, everyone in the pews turned in their own Bibles to follow along with him—not just the adults, but even the teenagers and children. I thought, "I've never seen anything like this in my life!"

So, for the next two weeks, I became a fanatic Catholic and Baptist at the same time. I attended Mass at St. Stanislaus on weekdays and Sunday mornings, and I made it to the Sunday morning worship services at the Baptist church, along with the Sunday night and Wednesday night meetings, too. I just wanted to find out what was going on there.

After two weeks of curious observation, I wanted to talk to the pastor. He was saying things that I had either not heard before or things that were a little different from what I had heard and been taught in the Catholic Church. I called him on the phone on a Sunday afternoon and arranged to meet with him after the evening service. I was afraid to go alone, so I took Lenore and Barbara with me.

There in his office Pastor Jordan began talking with me about what God had done in his life. I listened carefully, and as he spoke of God's mercy and grace, he made a statement that made me stop cold. "Wilma, I never knew I was bad enough to go to hell just by being born into this world, and nothing takes away the penalty of sin but the blood of Jesus Christ." As soon as he said that, I leaned forward and put my elbow on the edge of his desk. I started to point at him and opened my mouth, but no words came out. I was awestruck!

I kept staring at him in silence until finally he came to the point: "Wilma, would you like to ask Jesus to be your personal Savior?" I continued to stare at him with my mouth open and my finger pointing, eventually shaking my head, "No." He said, "Wilma, don't put it off. Right now you know that you are lost, and no one but Jesus can save you."

He went on to explain that it is not by works of righteousness which you do that gets you to heaven, but it's by God's mercy that He'll save you (Tit. 3:5). It's by grace that you are saved through faith, and not by anything you can do. It's God's gift, not something earned by your own works (Eph. 2:8-9). Nobody can go before Jesus when he dies and say, "Look what I did to get to heaven!" Jesus paid it all with His precious blood on the cross. Without the shedding of blood, there's no remission or forgiveness of sin (Heb. 9:22). He told me that my church wasn't going to get me to heaven; his Baptist church wasn't going to get him to heaven; nobody else's church is going to get them to heaven, either. Sin can only be forgiven by the blood of the Lamb, and Jesus Christ is the Lamb of God Who came to take away the sin of the world (Jn. 1:29). Then he said to me, "Wilma, Jesus died for you, but you have to accept His gift of salvation. I'm only going to ask you this last time, won't you please ask Jesus to be your personal Savior?"

I hadn't moved a muscle; I was still open-mouthed, staring, and pointing; but this time I managed to nod my head, "Yes!" At that moment the Holy Spirit helped me to understand my lost condition. I knew I wanted Christ to be my personal Savior. Pastor Jordan told me to bow my head and ask Jesus to forgive me for being a sinner, to give me the free gift of eternal life, and to take me to heaven when I die. It was 10:30 p.m., November 11, 1973, when I experienced the mercy of God. His love and compassion reached down to me in my sin and lifted that weight from my soul. I was forgiven, not because of what I had done, but because of what He had done for me!

A New Life

As soon as we were finished there in the pastor's office, Barbara Besch invited me to her house for some refreshments. I left there around midnight and went home to my Hatfield Village apartment. I knelt down next to my bed and started to pray. "God, I don't understand a lot of the things these people are talking about. But I do know one thing; I've got a lot of things in my life that are wrong, and I want to be different."

At that point the Lord brought to mind all the things I was doing wrong in my life—drinking heavily, smoking almost three packs of cigarettes a day, using a lot of swear words in my vocabulary, and dancing in the clubs. (I had been at the disco the night before.) At the same time He brought to my memory one of the Gospel readings from the Catholic Mass. (At every Mass there is a Gospel and an Epistle reading.) It was the prayer of Jesus in the Garden of Gethsemane the night before He was crucified: "Not my will, but Thine be done." There on my knees I prayed that prayer to God. "I don't want my will in my life anymore. I've made a mess of it for twenty-nine and a half years! Would You please make me different?"

That night I didn't know the verse, "if any man be in Christ, he is a new creature: old things are passed away; behold, all things are become new" (II Cor. 5:17), but that's exactly what happened in my life. When I got up the next morning, everything had changed. God's mercy and grace were at work, taking away my desire for drinking and smoking. The swearing was gone, and my music changed overnight. I had such a desire to sing songs to honor Him. Psalm 40:2-3 express my testimony, "He brought me up also out of an horrible pit, out of the miry

39

clay, and set my feet upon a rock, and established my goings. And he hath put a new song in my mouth, even praise to our God: many shall see it, and fear, and shall trust in the LORD." God took away the old habits and gave me new desires for my new life with Him.

My fellow workers and friends met the "new Wilma" with some skepticism, but they couldn't deny I had changed. The lawyers and secretaries at the Lansdale law firm where I had worked for six months before my salvation had gotten to know the old me, and they would have six and a half years to watch how God would work in my life. I worked with a number of Catholic secretaries there, and at break times I would tell them what had happened. Their reply was, "Wilma, you can't drink or smoke or dance now because you go to the Baptist church, and they won't let you do those things!" I answered that I could drink as much as I wanted to; I could smoke as much as I wanted to; I could dance as much as I wanted to. It's just that I didn't "want to" any more. Of course, the difference was that I had become a new creature in Christ with the Spirit of God dwelling in me. He had changed my desires and was constraining me with the love of Christ to please Him in all that I would do or say.

A week after I was saved, Steve, the man I had been dating for some time, took me out to the Wagon Wheel Restaurant, a place we had frequented before the Lord came into my life. When we were seated he ordered drinks for both of us, but I told him I didn't want one. Knowing well my past inclination, he didn't believe me and instructed the waitress to go ahead and bring the drinks. When she did, I took one sip of mine and put it back down on the table. It tasted horrible in my mouth, and I didn't touch another drop of it. About halfway through the meal, the waitress came back to ask if we wanted another round of drinks. When I indicated that I didn't want another one, Steve noticed that my first one was still sitting there, and he couldn't believe it. He said, "Wilma, you didn't drink your drink!" I told him that I hadn't wanted it in the first place. He said, "Of course you want that drink!" and then ordered another round for both of us. When we left the restaurant later, both of my drinks were still sitting there. When God took the alcohol out of my life, it was gone.

The Lord took the desires for drinking and smoking out of my life literally overnight. Nonetheless, He soon confirmed that the new life He gave me held no room for those old habits. I was well aware that drinking could make my mind fuzzy and break down my resistance to temptations. After I was saved, I realized that to willfully take such a substance into my body could prevent me from gaining victory over temptations through Christ's strength. I needed to choose His ways for my life, and alcohol could at any time make me incapable of that choice.

And when I considered the smoking, God reminded me of the medical research findings which had been published and reported by the news media. Researchers, even then, were saying that every cigarette a person smoked took time off of his life span. The health hazards were becoming obvious. I learned that I Cor. 6:19-20 says, "What? know ye not that your body is the temple of the Holy Ghost which is in you, which ye have of God, and ye are not your own? For ye are bought with a price: therefore glorify God in your body, and in your spirit, which are God's." My life was God's, and my body was God's. I saw that I didn't have a right to put anything into "His body" that would harm it or cause me to sin with it.

My new life in Christ was going to be different. I can't take any credit for the sudden turnaround in my desires and actions. It was purely God's mercy and grace at work. Romans 12:1-2 says, "I beseech you therefore, brethren, by the mercies of God, that ye present your bodies a living sacrifice, holy, acceptable unto God, which is your reasonable service. And be not conformed to this world: but be ye transformed by the renewing of your mind, that ye may prove what is that good, and acceptable, and perfect, will of God." As I continue on in my Christian life, I'm in constant need of His power to transform me as I yield myself to Him.

WORSHIPPING IN TRUTH

About six months before I had left the convent, I was kneeling at the altar rail to receive communion at Mass. As usual, the priest came up to me, held the host in front of me, and said, "The body of Christ." I was supposed to respond immediately with the word, "Amen." I had been taking communion for twenty years and had said "Amen" in response thousands of times. But at that Mass, for the first time, a thought raced through my head before I spoke the affirmation—"Is it really?" Is that wafer really the body of Christ? And every time I attended Mass after that, that same question seemed to pop into my thoughts. As I understood the teachings of my church at that time, it seemed that Jesus had to die at every Mass for sin—that His blood had to be shed again.

For clarification here, I need to explain that the Catholic Church clearly teaches the doctrine of Transubstantiation. This doctrine declares that in the Mass the bread and the wine are converted into the body and blood of Christ. In addition, the Church teaches that the Eucharist (communion) is a sacrifice. Technically, as I have learned since, it does not say that Jesus dies again at every Mass, but rather that the Eucharist "re-presents" the sacrifice of the cross. It is an ambiguous teaching that the Church itself labels a "mystery." In any case I, at that time, assumed (like many others) that the Church taught Christ was dying again at every Mass. And it was my doubts about Transubstantiation and the Mass sacrifice that posed the only questions I had about my Church's teachings.

Actually, I had talked to God about those matters while still there at the convent. I had said, "God, if that is Jesus in there (in the bread), show me it is. But if it's not, show me the truth." As a result of that prayer, I believe God led me all the way to an opportunity to find the answer. Once I was saved, the Holy Spirit of Truth, Who was now dwelling in me, quickly found occasion to bring it to my mind. God wanted me to find the truth about worshipping Him in the Bible, and so that question was about to send me on an unsettling crash course in true worship.

It began a few days after I was saved. While visiting at Lenore's house, she asked me how I was worshipping God. I told her, "Well, I'm Catholic, and I'm satisfied. Besides, I only have one question about my church, just one." She inquired what it was, and so I asked her, "Lenore, does Jesus need to die at every Mass for sin?" I was surprised at the certainty with which she answered that He didn't. When I asked how she knew, she told me that the Bible said so, and she took me right to the Scriptures. There in Hebrews 10:10-14 we read, ". . . the offering of the body of Jesus Christ once for all. And every priest standeth daily ministering and offering oftentimes the same sacrifices, which can never take away sins: But this man, after he had offered one sacrifice for sins for ever, sat down on the right hand of God. . . For by one offering he hath perfected for ever them that are sanctified." Then in verse 18 it adds, "there is no more offering for sin."

Lenore closed the Bible and asked me this: "Do you believe God can lie?" Of course I knew that God would be a sinner if He lied. So God couldn't lie, and I gave that reply. She went on to ask, "Do you believe that the Bible is God's Word?" Now at that time, if she would have asked me if I believed that every word in the Bible is God's word, I would have said no. As a Catholic, I was a "literary formist," believing that the Bible was God's word and a piece of literature with good stories, but not that every word is inspired by God. The way she asked the question, however, I could readily answer, "yes."

Then she came to the point. "Wilma, how many times did God say in the Bible that Jesus had to die for sin?" Hebrews 10:10 clearly said once. "And how many times does your church say He has to die for sin?" I knew the answer was every day at every Mass. I pointed my finger, opened my mouth, and sat there in silence the same way I had in Pastor Jordan's office a few nights before. Finally, Lenore said, "They're different, aren't they? Which one are you going to trust? God, Who can't lie or men who can make mistakes?"

Even though that one question catapulted me into an important examination of Scripture, the real heart of the matter before me was whether or not I could be saved and remain a Catholic. I told Lenore that day as I sat there dumbfounded by the truth I was seeing, "All I know is that I love God so much, I want to make sure He hears my worship." She assured me that if I truly wanted to know what was right, God would show me. So for about a week she took me through a Bible study to help me see what Scripture says about a lot of important matters.

Psalm 86:15 says, "But Thou, O Lord, art a God full of compassion, and gracious, long suffering, and plenteous in mercy and truth." I had experienced His mercy in salvation, but now it was time for me to learn more of His truth.

"God is a Spirit: and they that worship Him must worship Him in spirit and in truth" (John 4:24). When I accepted Jesus Christ as my Savior, His Holy Spirit came to dwell in me so that I could worship Him "in spirit." But how could I worship Him "in truth?" John 14:6 and 17:17 tell us that Jesus Himself is Truth and that God's

Word is truth. I had to find the truth about worship in the Christ of Scripture, and so does everyone else.

It's interesting for me to look back at my life and see that God had been preparing me for this look at Scripture for many years. When I was young I remember seeing my dad sitting and reading the Bible. Now that was before Vatican II, and the Church was still discouraging people from reading the Bible for themselves. I didn't think about what that meant then; I just knew I wanted to do anything my dad did. When I'd be cleaning in the den and see his Bible lying there, I'd open it and try to read it. At that time, though, all I would think about it was, "What's he get out of this?"

By the time I became a Sister of Mercy, however, the Vatican II changes began to encourage the people to read the Bible for themselves. In the convent it was required reading, so I bought my own Jerusalem Bible. Devotions, meditations, and even "Bible studies" brought me some familiarity with Scripture while a nun. But later, when I was saved, I had the Spirit of Truth to guide me into the truth of Scripture (John 16:13).

When Lenore and I began that Bible study, we looked at the other sacraments as taught by the Catholic Church: Baptism, Confirmation, Penance, Matrimony, Holy Orders, and Extreme Unction. We also dealt with topics like purgatory and prayer to Mary and the saints. As we studied, I saw that what the Bible was saying was not what my church had taught me. But, I didn't trust Lenore's Bible. I went and got the Catholic Bible to check out what it said. Both Lenore's Bible and the Catholic Bible agreed, saying the same things about those matters.

That's when I started to get scared. Over the course of the Bible study, it became clear to me that what the Catholic Church taught and what even the Catholic Bible said were not the same thing. Something was wrong, and so I decided that I had to get to a priest. Surely he would know the answer to this new conundrum I was facing.

Soon I was knocking at the front door of the Rectory of St. Stanislaus in Lansdale. Father Phil Ricci, my choir director, came to the door and greeted me. But when I said, "Father! I need to talk to you," he looked at his watch and indicated he was too busy right then. I couldn't wait, and so I blurted out, "Father Ricci! You've got to talk to me! I'm trying to salvage everything I have ever believed in the Catholic Church for twenty-nine and a half years. Please sit down and talk to me!"

He did sit down with me for about forty-five minutes. I shared with him all the questions I was facing, all the things I was being told, all the preaching I was hearing. I even tried to quote as much of the Bible as I could remember to illustrate my plight. He just sat there and listened to me talk—until I asked him to baptize me.

"Weren't you baptized as a baby?" he asked.

"Well, yes sir, I was, but I was only a month old when I was baptized. Saint Peter says in Acts 2:38 that you have to repent and be baptized. Father Ricci, I couldn't repent of anything. I didn't even know I was a sinner when I was a month old. But I did repent of my sins last week. I got saved, and now I need to get baptized."

At that point it was easy to see that he was getting upset. "Wilma," he said, "if you were baptized as a baby, that took away your original sin, made you a child of God, and an heir of heaven. You don't need to get baptized." I began to protest and tell him what the Bible says, but he stopped me and basically said that he didn't care what the Bible said.

Then Father Ricci made a statement that I won't forget. "Wilma, you will never leave the Catholic Church— never!" Considering the fact that he hadn't answered any of my questions, I asked him why he could say that. He replied, "Because you are too steeped in the traditions of the Church."

"Father Ricci!" I said, "I'm not looking for traditions in any church." I was looking for the truth, and I had found it in the Scriptures. The Spirit of Truth had started to teach me.

Nonetheless, Father Ricci gave me two recommendations that gave me some hope of resolving my situation. He told me to read the lives of the saints and to go to a Bible study that was being taught by a nun. The first bit of advice didn't help at all, but I was excited at the prospect of the second. I thought, "That's it! I'm going to be able to go and get some Catholic answers from the Bible so that I can use them against all these Baptists who are using the Bible with me."

I eagerly found out the details of when and where the study would meet, and I was there ready to learn when the meeting began. The nun taught the Epistle to the Romans—the one book that tells us about sin and its wages, about eternal life being (as my Catholic Bible says) "the free gift of God" (Rom. 6:23), about how to get that free gift, as well as about what our lives are like after we have that gift. She taught that study covering the entire book of Romans in one hour that night. In the process she missed every one of those important truths. She really had no idea what she was teaching.

(I later came to realize that, as sincere as that nun may have been, without the Spirit of Truth to guide her, she just didn't have the ability to understand those passages for herself. As I Corinthians 2:14 says, "But the natural man receiveth not the things of the Spirit of God: for they are foolishness unto him: neither can he know them, because they are spiritually discerned.")

So I left the Bible study that night as perplexed as ever. I still didn't have the answers. I kept going to Mass and to the Baptist services, all the time still asking God to show me the truth—to show me what was right. This was the hardest struggle I had ever faced. Everything I had believed and accepted throughout my life about worshipping God was now challenged. I had Scripture and I had man's opinions in front of me to sort out. What should I do?

Mercifully, God did not leave me in that confused state long. And, in His unique way, He chose to show me the truth at a Catholic Mass. For a few weeks I had been going to the Sunday morning Mass at St. Stanislaus, singing in the choir there, and then driving to the Baptist church for their morning worship service. But because the choir sang at different Masses, this particular Sunday I didn't have to go until 12:15. So I went to the Baptist service first, and then drove through town to the Catholic church. I sobbed all the way, pleading with the Lord to straighten out my conundrum. I couldn't keep going on like this.

At St. Stanislaus I climbed the stairs to the choir loft with the other singers and surveyed the familiar setting. It was a large church, probably holding about a thousand people for a Mass. There were beautiful long, narrow stained glass windows in the front of the church with a white marble wall between them. The altar, the platform on which it stood, and the steps leading up to it were all made of white marble as well. And hovering over that white scenery, suspended from the ceiling, was a black cross holding a white corpse of Christ.

As I looked down from the choir loft at the Consecration of the Mass that day, I saw things as I had never seen them before. Because of the angle of my view, when the priest elevated the host and the chalice during the Mass, I saw directly above them the eyes of Jesus on the cross. The priest said, "This is my body," raising the host, and it was as if Jesus Himself was saying to me right then,

"Wilma, I don't need to be on this cross. I don't need to be in this bread. I died 'once for all!'" Then as the priest held up the chalice to say, "This is my blood," it happened again. "Wilma, I don't need to shed my blood any more. It was shed 'once for all!'"

Tears were rolling down my face, but they weren't tears of sorrow. They were tears of joy and relief. The Lord had made it plain to me that Jesus Christ does not need to die at every Mass for sins. At that point I knew that the Bible was true and that the Church was wrong. Overjoyed that God had revealed this truth to me, I knelt there, and when it was time for communion, I didn't go up to the priest and receive it.

The service wasn't over, however, and the Lord added a final note of celebration to my answered prayer. At the end of each Mass the priest and servers would gather at the foot of the altar and then leave to go to the sacristy while the congregation sang a recessional song. At the close of that song, the congregation would turn around to listen to our choir sing one more hymn. That day the choir sang "The Battle Hymn of the Republic." "Mine eyes have seen the glory of the coming of the Lord! His truth is marching on!" I sang that song with a new-found joy and freedom, and I left Mass at St. Stanislaus for the last time.

Choices and Challenges

Settling the issue about communion with the truth of Scripture also determined for me where I had to find the truth for all other matters of faith. I couldn't really trust people and traditions any more. I had to go to God's Word for myself and find out what He really said. So I became a "Berean Christian"—searching the Scriptures daily to see if the things people were telling me were true (Acts 17:11). Then, as I saw the truth, I had to act.

My friends at Calvary Baptist—Lenore, Barbara, and Anita—were faithfully telling me that I needed to be baptized. And, as I had studied with Lenore, I found the Bible describes baptism as an outward expression of the inward repentance that has taken place in a believer (Acts 2:41; 8:26-39; 16:25-34). Scripture just didn't support Catholicism's claim that the rite of baptism takes away original sin and makes a person a child of God and an heir of heaven. I knew I had to be obedient to God's Word, but to get baptized again was an awfully big and difficult step for a life-long devout Catholic like me. It would be taking a stand against everything I had been taught and had believed.

God was once again showing mercy to me. Because of my surgery in October (just prior to my salvation), I was not supposed to be immersed in water for the next six weeks. That restriction was the Lord's way of putting a little "fence" around me to protect me from being pressured into a quick decision on baptism. But when the time was up, the Holy Spirit had convinced me of what I had to do, and God gave me peace about it. I was baptized and joined Calvary Baptist Church the next Sunday evening, December 16.

On Christmas Eve I went home to spend the holiday with my family. When I told my mother that I had trusted Christ as my Savior and that I was no longer a Catholic, she was, needless to say, stunned. After all, I was the girl who had always wanted to be a nun and who was a truly devout Catholic. How could it be that I had left the Church? Looking back on it, I know that was quite a blow to level at my family. At least I had several weeks to deal with my salvation and all the changes God was bringing into my life. Now I was springing it on them all at once.

I did agree to go with my mom to the Christmas Mass at SS. Peter & Paul Roman Catholic Church, where we sat with other family members. As I listened to the Mass, the Holy Spirit seemed to open my eyes to both the truth and the error in the liturgy that I had heard so often. In just six weeks of Bible study as a Christian, God had shown me enough truth to discern when the prayers and recitations were Scriptural and when they weren't. The verses He brought to my mind during that Mass reconfirmed what I knew to be true and gave me a real peace about the step I had taken.

When it had come time to receive communion in the past, I had always been the first person out of the pew and down the aisle to the altar rail. But not this time—I didn't move! That's when the rest of my family found out that I was no longer a Catholic. Of course, they were as shocked as my mom had been. I provided quite a Christmas surprise!

Those first few weeks and months of my Christian life were full of ups and downs. Most of the downs came in my old relationships. My boyfriend, Steve, couldn't comprehend the change in me, and we broke up. Most of my close friends were devout Catholics, and they abandoned me. And my family just didn't understand yet. It could have been a time of terrible loneliness and depression, but the Lord directed my new Christian friends to step in.

Lenore, Barbara, Anita, and others from church constantly included me in their plans. They invited me to dinners, parties, and fellowships. They opened their homes to me and made themselves available to answer my questions. Their love and concern encouraged me as a new child of God and gave me needed spiritual and emotional support. Their gracious care for me during that time was another marvelous example of God's mercy in my life.

I had been "talking to God" for years, but I didn't really begin to understand prayer until after my salvation. I was always taught that prayer was to be very formal and repetitious, even if I did offer spontaneous cries to God at times. But as I began to read the Scriptures, I found that Jesus said in Matthew 6:6-7 that when we pray, we are to go into our closet and pray. We're not to use vain repetitions, but to talk to our Father in secret, and He will hear us and reward us openly. He will communicate with us. Now I know I can just talk to Him as I did so naively as a child. He's right here with me saying, "Just talk to Me. I understand. I know. I'm the One you're supposed to talk to. Worship Me." As the Holy Spirit continued to show me the teachings of God's Word on prayer, that blessed communion with my Lord was certainly no longer a repetitious religious exercise.

I needed the wisdom and truth of Scripture, the consolation of prayer, and the support of Christian friends for many of the decisions I found myself making as a new Christian. Just before I was saved I had been approved as a Girl Scout leader. I was assigned my own troop in Lansdale, Pennsylvania, and the weekly meetings were held on Wednesday nights. Once I was saved, I had to make a decision about which meeting I was going to attend—the Girl Scout meetings or the Wednesday evening service at church. It was hard to turn my back on the Girl Scouts, but I knew I needed the spiritual food and fellowship of meeting with other Christians.

My work at the law firm—Pearlstine, Salkin, Hardiman & Robinson—presented plenty of challenges to my faith. I naturally wanted to tell the people there at the office about the Lord, and I used appropriate opportunities to do a lot of witnessing. It didn't take long for me to get a reputation. My co-workers began warning all the visitors and new workers about me. "Don't talk to Wilma about religion because she will preach to you." As a result, many of the people there shied away from me, and the rejection wasn't easy to take. But as the months and years passed, I saw that a number of my co-workers began to come to me when difficult situations arose in their lives. When they had problems, they opened up to me and wanted me to pray for them. I even had the precious opportunity of leading a few of them to the Lord.

One interesting witnessing experience that came up at the law firm involved an IBM trainer. We had purchased some new equipment from IBM, and they sent a lady to train me on how to use it. Before she began the training, she was "warned" about me. We had just gotten started that morning, when one of the attorneys, Larry, came into my office. He told us that he had a brief that needed to be done immediately. The trainer looked at him in amazement and said, "She just learned how to turn on the equipment!"

"That's good!" he said. "Now teach her how to do the rest, because we've got to have this brief for the judge by this afternoon."

We worked hard and without complaint to comply with Larry's demand. When we were finished, she remarked, "You know, I've heard a lot about you, and I'm probably going to end up getting saved!" I looked at her and said, "Yeah, you probably will!" I took her to lunch, and she indeed did trust the Lord as her Savior.

Probably the most difficult circumstance that came up at the law office was one that put a personal conviction of mine to the test. I worked for some time as secretary to one of the lawyers, George, who dealt primarily in eminent domain law. Therefore, I typed up many legal documents involving the government acquisition of private property. But then the firm's attorney who had handled all of the domestic cases, including divorces, left the firm. All of his cases were distributed to the remaining attorneys.

When I realized that George now had some of the divorce cases and I would be typing notes of testimony and other reports for their cases, I was deeply convicted. I knew that the Bible said, "What therefore God hath joined together, let not man put asunder" (Matt. 19:6). I really felt as if I were helping people get divorces by typing their papers, and I couldn't do that. So I went first to the office manager and explained to her my problem with typing those notes. Her reply was simply, "That's part of your job!" But when I told her that I would be resigning if I had to work with divorce cases, I soon found myself in the office of the senior partner, Jules Pearlstine.

Instead of pressuring me, Jules asked me not to quit but rather to take a position operating some new word processing equipment for the firm. I readily agreed, stopped working for George, and took the training from Olivetti for the new equipment. Then I got it set up and running to meet the office's demands. Unfortunately, I soon realized that one of the functions for that equipment involved notes of testimony for divorce proceedings. I thought the test of my conviction was over, but now the same problem had returned.

I went straight to Larry's office. He was the attorney in charge of determining the priority for all work assignments on the equipment. "Larry! You knew my conviction. Why didn't you tell me before I even started in this position that I would have to do notes of testimony?" He didn't say anything. He just gave me a sheepish grin.

While Larry and I were looking at each other, I thought, "Wilma, when you take a stand on something for the Lord, you'd better be willing to remain firm." I tendered my resignation that day, but Larry and the office manager asked me not to quit. They said they would find someone else to do the divorce work. That concession caused an uproar with the other secretaries, because I was refusing to do part of my work. Another girl, however, was willing to handle those matters, and everything worked out. In fact, I believe the Lord blessed me for being willing to stand on my convictions. The firm gave me three raises in pay that year—one for being willing to learn the equipment, one for making it work for the firm, and an extra one as commendation for my year's work.

Making difficult choices and facing challenges as a Christian is not always fun, but the Lord's mercies are always there to sustain us along life's way. And I am so thankful He has given us His Word as a lamp for our feet and a light for our path (Ps. 119:105).

New Mercies

Lamentations 3:22-23 says that, "It is of the LORD's mercies that we are not consumed, because His compassions fail not. They are new every morning: great is Thy faithfulness." As I now look back across more than five decades of my life, I marvel at God's faithfulness. I see His wondrous mercy at work, not only in my salvation, but all along my life's path. I needed the mercy I found at the cross that night in 1973, but I also need His "new mercies" every morning.

Perhaps the first of God's mercies to me was putting me in a wonderful family. My Mom and Dad loved and cared for me and my three sisters and one brother. There was no doubt about that. They set good examples for us: they worked hard; they provided for us; they were good friends and neighbors in the community; and they were there for their children. My dad, Jimmy Sullivan, worked two jobs to provide for all of us. The main job was at the Towanda Post Office, where he was the Superintendent of Mails. He held that position until his death in 1962. My mom, Vivian, worked as a nurse.

One of the things my dad did while I was growing up that left a lasting impression on me was washing the dishes on Sunday afternoons. We girls had that chore during the week, but on Sunday afternoons, Dad would insist it was his turn. He'd tune in a ball game on TV, and then head into the kitchen to wash a few dishes during every break in the action. He'd still be wiping a dish when he came out to watch the next inning or quarter. It would take him all afternoon to get the dishes done that way, but he wanted to do it for us. When some of his men friends would tease him about doing the dishes, he just told them that it kept his hands soft after working with paper all week at the post office.

Sports were so important to me as I was growing up, and I really appreciated the fact that Mom and Dad both allowed and supported my interest. When I'd come home from school, I'd holler to Mom, who was usually in the kitchen, "Hi, Mom!" And she'd respond with, "Hi, Wilma!" I'd run upstairs and change my clothes, and then head back downstairs and holler, "I'm going to play baseball!" or basketball, football, or whatever sport was in season. Though it wasn't much of a conversation, it was so good to know Mom was there and she cared about what I did.

If I wasn't playing competitive sports at school with the Girls Athletic Club (I was the president one year), I was out playing with the neighborhood kids. Unlike my older sisters, Sharon, Pat, and Marilyn, I was a tomboy and loved playing with my younger brother, Lee. I was his catcher, his end in football, and his basketball buddy. In whatever sport he and the kids played, I'd fill any position that was needed. The neighborhood boys nicknamed me "George," and that was fine with me. I walked around with my baseball glove on my belt, and I had my bat and cap ready to play whenever anybody got up a game.

Not only did we play sports—at home Lee and I would "play church." Sometimes he was the priest and I was the altar girl; other times I was the priest and he was the altar boy.

Undoubtedly, the most important thing my family did for me as I was growing up was to teach me that I needed to worship God. Ours was a good Catholic family. We always attended Sunday Mass, and Dad with his wonderful tenor voice sang solos in the church choir on special occasions like Easter. Of course I didn't find out the truth about salvation when I was growing up, but God still used that early influence at home to set my desires on a course that led me to His mercy.

I've already expressed the fact that the nuns at St. Agnes and my superiors in the convent had a positive impact on my life. The moral influence I gained from them and at home helped keep me out of trouble. And the Lord used those devoted ladies to teach me many valuable lessons for my life.

Of course God brought the circumstances together that put me with Lenore and the other folks at Calvary Baptist just when He was ready to bring me to the end of my self-efforts for peace and security. Then I knew what it was to say with the Psalmist, "I have trusted in Thy mercy; my heart shall rejoice in Thy salvation" (Ps. 13:5).

That most important turning point in life was followed by new mercies. God's mercies got me through the early trials in my Christian life. He took away the bad habits and gave me grace to deal with the unsettling changes in my life and relationships. In that display of His love and care, He began to show me that my new-found relationship with Him was something more precious than I could imagine!

In fact, the exploration of that new relationship has led me on a journey of over twenty-three years. I must confess that I haven't always stayed on the right track, though I could never escape His lovingkindness. One of the biggest stumbling blocks that has often tripped me up and kept me from a closer walk with my dear Savior springs from an old attribute of mine: wanting to serve.

Oh, I knew when I accepted Christ as my Savior that I could do nothing to save myself. The penalty for my sins was paid in full by the Lord Jesus Christ on the cross. I knew my good works were worthless to pay for my sin debt. I had to trust solely in Him and His gift of salvation (Eph. 2:8-9; Tit. 3:5-6). As a born-again Christian, my natural response was to want to serve my Lord Who died for me. Now, that response is good and right, but in the course of serving God it can become very easy for a Christian to grow more concerned with "what he does" than with "Whom he knows." When that happens, a Christian can fall into a trap of trying to "earn" an on-going relationship with Christ.

As a new Christian I became very active in reading my Bible, in witnessing to people, in participating in church activities, in doing all the right things and not doing all the wrong things just like a good Christian should. In 1980, God moved me to South Carolina where I got involved in more church work and Christian ministry. The Lord started opening doors for me to speak to ladies groups, and He was using my testimony in person and in tract form to touch the hearts of people. He gave me the opportunity to work with some other former priests and nuns who had come to know Christ as "the Way, the Truth, and the Life," and we shared our faith in books and videos. Then He opened the door for me to begin a teaching ministry with ladies across the country.

I was a missionary with Gospel Outreach out of Philadelphia, Pennsylvania, from 1988-91. Then I organized Phebe Ministries as the channel for my work with ladies in teaching and outreach. I was a busy Christian, and I found myself talking to countless other busy Christian ladies across the land, speaking at retreats, seminars, banquets, and Bible studies. I was stressing all the things we should do or shouldn't do to please the Lord. But it wasn't until June of 1991, while based in South St. Paul, Minnesota, that I finally began to understand the true meaning of mercy for my life as a Christian.

I was leading the adult ladies class during vacation

Bible school (VBS) at my church, and I noticed that one of the ladies would not look at me while I was teaching. As I was having my devotions the next morning, the Lord brought her to my mind. I began to think that maybe I had offended her in some way. If I had, I needed to go to her and be reconciled, and so I went by her home that morning. We chatted a few minutes, and then I brought up the fact that I had observed her reluctance to look at me while I was teaching, not only in VBS, but any time I had been speaking during my two years at that church. When she hesitated to say anything, I asked her to be transparent with me. Finally she said, "Wilma, you're not teaching what Pastor is teaching!"

I was shocked beyond words. "What did you say?" I asked, and she repeated her statement. I could only reply, "Polly, talk to me! What are you talking about?" For the next four hours she did talk to me while I sat there dumbfounded and in tears.

"Wilma, you've been teaching ladies here and around this country to 'do, do, do.' Wilma, you're wrong! You have the cart before the horse. It's not 'do, do, do' that God wants from us—it's to 'be' right with Him. Then He will 'do' through you what He wants done!" She continued on, sharing with me what the Lord had taught her about brokenness and revival in her own life, using Ezekiel 16 and Revelation 3.

When I left her home that afternoon I was drained and broken. I arrived home and walked next door to see my pastor at the church. He listened to me intently and confirmed everything Polly had shared with me. I asked him a question I had asked Polly earlier: "What am I going to teach tonight at VBS?" He said the same thing she had: "I guess you'll just have to ask the Lord about that."

In only one hour I had to begin teaching that ladies' class. I went before the throne of grace to obtain the mercy

61

and to find the grace to help in this great time of need! (Heb. 4:16). I picked up my outline for the lecture that evening, and the subject was that of abiding in Christ from John 15:1-5. At that point the Lord started to teach me anew about my personal relationship with Him.

Over these past six years I have come to understand more fully what Polly was saying to me there in her home in Minnesota. By His mercy and grace, the Lord has taught me with much lovingkindness and long-suffering about who I am in Him and what my new identity in Him is all about. I have come to realize that I am totally "accepted in the Beloved," and I am learning how that acceptance allows me now to have an intimate moment-by-moment relationship with Him. His acceptance of me is not based on my behavior—what I do or don't do for Him, but rather on my new birth into His family by faith alone in Christ's precious blood.

Christ didn't just change my desires when I got saved; He changed me. I was dead in sin; now I'm alive in Christ. My new identity is simply that I am "in Christ!" He has become my life, "for in Him [I] live, and move, and have [my] being" (Acts 17:28). Colossians 3:4 states that Christ is my life! I am not just a sinner saved by grace. I am a child of God who has the life of Christ at the very center of my being.

Understanding my identity in Christ does not mean that I am sinlessly perfect now. It has, in a deeper sense, made my sinfulness more real to me. As I've been asking the Lord to show me what He meant when He said in John 3:16 that God so loved me, He's been teaching me through His Word that He does not show me my sinfulness to make me feel like a worm. Revelation 4:11 says that He created me for His pleasure, and the Scripture declares that in His presence there is "fullness of joy" and that the "joy of the Lord" is my strength (Ps. 16:11,

Neh. 8:10). The reason He is showing me my sin is not for condemnation (Rom:8:1), but rather to reveal to me what He accomplished on the cross. He was made to become sin for me, though He knew no sin, that I "might be made the righteousness of God in Him" (II Cor 5:21).

From this new perspective, I'm not a sinner any more in the old sense—I'm a saint who may make wrong choices. I'm still responsible for those choices, but I'm not weighed down by guilt and condemnation. That may seem like a small matter of semantics, but to the Christian struggling with sin, it's a liberating truth. All of my sin—past, present, and future—was washed as white as snow by Christ's blood. God sees no sin in me. He sees Christ in me, and He loves me perfectly. When I understand that, my natural desire is to love Him in return, and that's exactly what He wants. Knowing Him and what He's done for me results in a relationship of love. And where there's true love for God, there is obedience to Him (Jn. 14:15,23).

There are so many wonderful Scripture passages that tell me more about the life I now have in Him. He was made unto me "wisdom, and righteousness, and sanctification, and redemption" (I Cor. 1:30). I am now dead and my "life is hid with Christ in God" (Col. 3:3), and "I am crucified with Christ: nevertheless I live: yet not I, but Christ liveth in me: and the life which I now live in the flesh I live by the faith of the Son of God, Who loved me, and gave Himself for me" (Gal. 2:20). It is Christ in me which is "the hope of glory" (Col. 1:27), and I am "complete in Him!" (Col. 2:10).

When the Holy Spirit started to reveal to me who I am in Christ, I was thrilled! As He continues to show me my "flesh" and how it is so contrary to my new nature and identity in Him, I want always to reckon myself "to be dead indeed unto sin, but alive unto God through Jesus

Christ our Lord" (Rom 6:11), and to yield every part of myself as "servants to righteousness unto holiness" (Rom 6:19).

You see, I still can [and should] serve God and enjoy doing it. I just have to realize that Christ has to work through me. My own efforts don't mean anything. Those years of trying to serve God in the convent could never work me into heaven. Christ's work at Calvary was all I needed, and His finished work is still all I need. Galatians 3:3, "Are ye so foolish? having begun in the Spirit, are ye now made perfect by the flesh?" helped drive that point home to me. I must be as dependent on Him now in my daily walk as a Christian as I was when I saw my need of salvation, because without Him I "can do nothing" (Jn. 15:5). The realization of that fact puts all the emphasis of the Christian life on my relationship with my Lord instead of on my activity. In that relationship alone, I can find a peace and satisfaction that can't be found anywhere else.

No matter what the years ahead may hold, I know the Lord's mercies are sure. I can be confident in His salvation and in the certainty of His constant love and care. How merciful God has been to me! And how thankful I am for His mercy and grace that have reached out to meet all of my need! "O give thanks unto the LORD, for He is good: for His mercy endureth for ever!" (Ps. 107:1).

A Personal Invitation

If after reading this book you realize that you have never accepted God's free gift of eternal life—or if you simply are not sure that you are in Christ—I invite you to receive Him right now. I never knew that going to heaven is a free gift. I always thought that I had to believe all the facts about Jesus and that I also had to do things to work my way to heaven. God said in His Word that it's "not by works of righteousness which we have done, but according to His mercy He saved us, by the washing of regeneration, and renewing of the Holy Spirit; which He shed on us abundantly through Jesus Christ our Savior" (Titus 3:5-6). God also said, "For by grace are you saved through faith; and that not of yourselves: it is the gift of God: not of works, lest any man should boast" (Ephesians 2:8-9).

Salvation is a free gift that you accept by faith. A suggested prayer for asking Jesus Christ for His forgiveness and free gift of eternal life is:

Lord Jesus, thank You for dying in my place on the cross to pay the penalty for my sins. Please forgive me and give me Your free gift of salvation. As a new, born-again child of God, please teach me more about Your love and grace and about my relationship with You. Take my life and make me into the person You want me to be. Amen.

If you have received Jesus Christ through reading this book or if you would like more information, I would appreciate hearing from you. May God bless you with a deep personal understanding and experience of His match-less love, grace, and mercy!

My mailing address is:

Wilma Sullivan
P. O. Box 16734
Greenville, SC 29606 USA

ADDITIONAL REFERENCE MATERIALS

BOOKS

The Gospel According to Rome
by James McCarthy

This powerful and insightful examination of the Catholic Church provides:
- a side-by-side comparison of Scripture with the first new world-wide Catholic catechism in four hundred years
- a summary of how modern Catholicism views grace, works, and heaven
- twenty-four ways the Catholic plan of salvation still stands in contrast to biblical truth
- a balanced overview of how the authority structure of the Roman Catholic Church compares with that of the New Testament church

Protestants and Catholics: Do They Now Agree?
by John Ankerberg and John Weldon

Can Protestants and Catholics truly unite? Ankerberg and Weldon answer that question by expertly evaluating the current teachings of the Catholic Church in the light of God's Word. Christians will find this book a valuable source of discernment and guidance as they determine how to respond to today's efforts to unite Catholics and Protestants.

The Facts on Roman Catholicism
by John Ankerberg and John Weldon

Authors Ankerberg and Weldon offer a biblical examination of Catholic doctrine and provide important insight into this influential religion.

C.E.N.T.
by Frank Eberhardt

The *Catholicism Explained New Testament* is dedicated to Roman Catholic people everywhere. This is more than a Scripture text; it is a helpful research guide and study guide that will aid your understanding and allow you to grow in godliness.

Many verses are followed by an italicized section. This means that there is a useful explanation of the text. This material is taken from Catholic doctrine and tradition and is compared to the context or meaning of the passage. Often the outcome makes you think and, if you wonder what the rest of Scripture teaches, handy cross-references have been provided to help you follow the thought through to a conclusion. There are more study aids in the front introduction (in a question and answer format) and in the back index (references list by topic.)

VIDEO

Catholicism: Crisis of Faith
by James G. McCarthy

This fast-moving video documentary examines the post-Vatican II Roman Catholic Church through interviews with former and practicing priests and nuns. It is an ideal resource for churches, Bible schools, mission agencies, or anyone interested in understanding modern Roman Catholicism. Gentle enough to share with Catholic friends and neighbors, Catholicism: Crisis of Faith is also a proven evangelistic tool. Available in English, Spanish, Portuguese, Polish, and Korean. To purchase, contact your local Christian video distributor, or write to:

Phebe Ministries, Inc.
P. O. Box 16734
Greenville, SC 29606 USA

New Mercies
Recommended Book List

Hession, Roy
The Calvary Road (Fort Washington, PA: Christian Literature Crusade, 1950).

We Would See Jesus (Fort Washington, PA: Christian Literature Crusade, 1950).

Murray, Andrew
Abide in Christ (Springdale, PA: Whitaker House, 1979).

Like Christ (Springdale, PA: Whitaker House, 1983).

The Master's Indwelling (Minneapolis, MN: Bethany House Publishers, 1977).

Nee, Watchman
Christ, the Sum ao All Spiritual Things (New York, NY: Christian Fellowship Publishers, Inc., 1973).

The Normal Christian Life (Wheaton, IL: Tyndale House Publishers, Inc. 1977).

Smith, Hannah Whitall
The Christian's Secret of a Happy Life (Springdale, PA: Whitaker House, 1983).

Thomas, W. Ian
The Saving Life of Christ (Grand Rapids, MI: Zondervan Publishing House, 1961).

Tozer, A.W.

The Knowledge of the Holy (San Francisco, CA: Harper Collins Publishers, 1961).

The Pursuit of God (Camp Hill, PA: Christian Publishers, 1982).

Wilma's mother, Vivian, when she graduated from nursing school at the Robert Packer School of Nursing in Sayre, Pennsylvania.

Wilma's dad, Jimmy Sullivan's, graduation picture from high school.

Wilma and her father and mother on the day she received her First Holy Communion at SS. Peter & Paul Roman Catholic Church in Towanda. Pennsylvania in May of 1951.

Parochial School, Towanda, Pa.

St. Agnes Parochial School in Towanda, Pennsylvania where Wilma attended for her first seven years of education. Photo compliments of Henry G. Farley.

A second grade picture of Wilma as a student at St. Agnes Parochial School in Towanda, Pennsylvania.

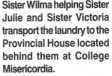

Sister Wilma helping Sister Julie and Sister Victoria transport the laundry to the Provincial House located behind them at College Misericordia.

Sister Wilma Marie, R.S.M.—a picture taken in Harrisburg, Pennsylvania while she taught at Our Lady of the Blessed Sacrament Catholic School in 1969–1971.

Wilma's graduation picture from Towanda Valley Joint Jr./Sr. High School in Towanda, Pennsylvania in 1962.

SS Peter & Paul Roman Catholic Church in Towanda, Pennsylvania, the church in which Wilma was raised. Photo compliments of Henry G. Farley.

Right Reverend Monsignor Joseph A. Griffin, Ph.D., V.F., the priest who was in charge of SS Peter & Paul Roman Catholic Church in Towanda, Pennsylvania while Wilma was growing up. Photo compliments of Henry G. Farley.

The original habit worn by the Sisters of Mercy. Photo compliments of Henry G. Farley.

St. Agnes Chapel where Wilma cleaned and assisted the nuns while growing up. Photos compliments of Henry G. Farley.

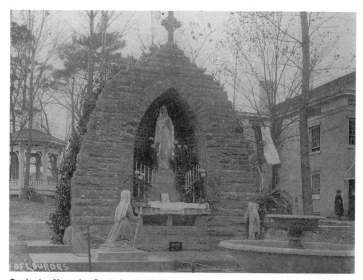

Our Lady of Lourdes Grotto located in Towanda, Pennsylvania next to St. Agnes School and the Sisters of Mercy Convent. Wilma participated in ceremonies there during the month of May for the crowning of Mary during her special month which was set aside for her. Photo compliments of Henry G. Farley.

Sisters of Mercy Convent in Towanda, Pennsylvania.

The three ladies who befriended and discipled Wilma after her salvation on November 11, 1973. Pictured are: Barbara Besch, Wilma, Anita Wetzel, and Lenore Dickinson.

Mrs. Patricia (Polly) Newborg who confronted Wilma about her teachings while living in Minnesota. Photo used by permission of Olan Mills.

Wilma teaching ladies at a retreat on behalf of Phebe Ministries, Inc. in Louisiana in 1997.

Co-author Pam Creason with children.